This book
belongs to:

M
Jackso███████████

Disney

5-Minute Stories

FRIENDSHIP

By Augusto Macchetto and Paola Mulazzi
Adapted by Lara Bergen

Disney PRESS

New York

Artwork for *Dumbo*: pencils by Kim Raymond, colors by Jody Daily

Artwork for *The Little Mermaid*: pencils by Marco Colletti, colors by Maria Elena Naggi

Artwork for *The Lion King*: pencils by Manuela Razzi, colors by Andrea Cagol

Artwork for *Mulan*: pencils by Mario Cortés, colors by Rae Ecklund and Robert Steele

Artwork for *The Aristocats*: pencils by Alan Batson, colors by Mara Dimiani and Silvano Scolari

Original title: *Un Mondo di Amicizia—Racconti per stare insieme*
Copyright © 2003 Disney

5-Minute Stories: Friendship
Copyright © 2005 Disney Enterprises, Inc.

The Aristocats is based on the book by Thomas Rowe.

Printed in the United States of America

First Edition

1 3 5 7 9 10 8 6 4 2

Library of Congress Catalog Card number: 2004112599

ISBN 0-7868-3606-7

Visit www.disneybooks.com

Contents

DUMBO

A Tail Tale

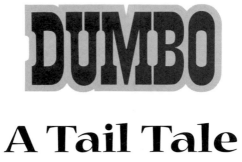

Dumbo and Timothy Mouse had made a new friend. His name was Eeny, and he lived at the circus with his brothers Meeny, Miny, and Mo. And just like Dumbo, with his great big ears, Eeny also had a certain something special about him: a very, very, *very* long tail!

Now, Dumbo and Timothy Mouse knew
that just because you had big ears—or a
long tail—it didn't mean you weren't as
good as everybody else. Everyone is special
in their own way. But Eeny's brothers were
not as open-minded, and they teased the
poor monkey every chance they got.

One day, Eeny's brothers even tied his tail to a tent pole. They laughed
and laughed and laughed until their little monkey sides were sore.
    Luckily for Eeny, Dumbo and Timothy Mouse came along to untie him.

"I wish my tail was just like every other monkey's," Eeny said with a sigh.

"Don't be silly," said Timothy. "Your tail is terrific. Isn't it, Dumbo?"

Dumbo nodded, flapping his great big ears.

"My brothers don't think so," said Eeny. "They're always making fun of me."

"Well, we sure know what that's like. Don't we, Dumbo?" said Timothy Mouse. "You know, Eeny, before you came to the circus, there was a time when everyone made fun of Dumbo, too," he explained.

"But why?" Eeny asked, surprised. Everyone knew that Dumbo was a star act!

Dumbo wiggled his ears.

"Why, because of those tent flaps he's got for ears," Timothy answered. "In fact, for a while, no one would even talk to him. But then we showed 'em that these big old special ears could do big old special things."

"Like fly!" said Eeny.

"Exactly," said Timothy.

"But my tail can't help me fly," Eeny said sadly.

"No," said Timothy. "But I bet it can do some other pretty spectacular things."

"I doubt it," replied Eeny gloomily.

"Well, first you've got to cheer up!" exclaimed Timothy.

Dumbo nodded and tootled a happy little tune, playing his trunk like a horn.

Eeny brightened up. "Say, that's not bad!" he cried. Holding his tail like a string bass, he plucked it to get a tune. *Thumpa-thumpa-thumpa-thump!* Together, he and Dumbo continued their song.

Right away, Meeny, Miny, and Mo ran up to investigate. "Hey! It's Eeny!" they cried. "He's making music with his tail!"

Miny and Mo loved Eeny's musical tail. They cheered and clapped when Eeny and Dumbo finished their song. But Eeny's other brother, Meeny, was not so quick to change his ways. He was used to making fun of Eeny. He was not used to *having* fun with Eeny.

"What's so great about thumpa-thumpa-thumping a tail?" he muttered to himself.

"Hey, Dumbo," said Timothy Mouse, "grab the end of Eeny's tail and let's see what else Eeny can do. Ready, Eeny? Okay, guys—jump!"

Holding the tip of Eeny's long tail in his trunk, Dumbo twirled it around and around like a jump rope. Happily, Miny and Mo leaped right in.

"This is great!" Miny exclaimed.

"Yeah, Eeny!" said Mo. "You've got a built-in jump rope!"

But where was Meeny?

Suddenly, they heard a yell coming from inside the big top.

"Hey, everybody! Look at me! Look what I can—HELP!"

Eeny, Miny, and Mo ran into the tent, followed by Timothy Mouse and Dumbo. There was Meeny, hanging by the tip of his tail from the highest trapeze. He had been jealous of Eeny, and he had wanted to show everyone what he could do with *his* tail. But his trick hadn't gone exactly as planned.

"Help me!" Meeny called out again. "I'm going to fall!"

"Dumbo," Timothy Mouse cried, "we've got to fly up there!"

But before Dumbo's ears could even start flapping, Eeny had scaled the tent pole and was lowering his tail to his frightened brother.

"It's okay!" Eeny shouted. "Just grab my tail and I'll pull you up."

Meeny did as he was told, and a few minutes later, the two monkeys were safe on solid ground.

"Boy, am I lucky to have such a brave brother," Meeny said with a sigh.

That afternoon, in honor of their brother the hero, Meeny, Miny, and Mo put on a tail-band concert of their own. And from that day on, they never, ever made fun of Eeny's long, long tail again.

Ariel's Peace

One day, as Ariel and Flounder were passing by the throne room, they heard King Triton speaking to a few of his bravest soldiers.

"The humans," he announced, "are building boats!"

Humans! Ariel thought. She knew that her father believed these land dwellers were very dangerous. But to Ariel they were mysterious and fascinating. She stopped swimming to hear what else her father had to say.

"Humans use their boats to capture sea creatures," King Triton continued. "For this reason, I am sending you to the coast to see how many boats they have and how great a danger they pose to our people."

Immediately, the king's soldiers gathered up their tridents and headed for the coast.

"Come on!" Ariel told Flounder. "We're going with them!"

"But, Ariel," Flounder protested, "what's your father going to say?"

"Nothing," Ariel said with a smile, "because he's never going to know!"

Even from a distance, it was clear that the humans were hard at work. Some of the men were building a boat near the shore. Others were on land, gathering grain. A few were fishing with big nets.

Hiding among the nearby rocks, Ariel gazed with amazement at the rippling golden fields. How different it all was from the world she knew. And how beautiful!

Triton's soldiers headed toward the shore to observe the villagers more closely. Ariel and Flounder followed.

Suddenly, Ariel saw that one of King Triton's soldiers was in trouble. He was caught in a fishing net!

"We've been ambushed!" cried the soldier as the net closed around him. "Forget about me!" he called to his comrades. "Save yourselves!"

But a mer-soldier never leaves another behind. Tridents in hand, they swam toward their friend.

Needless to say, the fisherman was dumbstruck when he heaved his net onto shore—and saw not fish, but a furious merman. He was even more shocked when a small army of mer-soldiers emerged from the sea. The fisherman called to his friends in the fields for help. Grabbing their pitchforks, the farmers raced to defend their comrade.

Where the land met the sea, humans met mer-soldiers face-to-face and ready to fight. As Ariel watched, she knew she had to stop them.

"Wait!" she exclaimed.

To both sides' surprise, Ariel swam between them. She grabbed a trident from an astonished soldier's hand. Before anyone could stop her, she swam up to the human.

"We come as friends," she declared, offering up the trident. "These are gifts for you. Your tools have wooden tines and can easily break. But these are made of steel. They will last forever—just as the peace between our peoples should be everlasting."

The mer-soldiers watched the farmer lay down his pitchfork and smile as he gently took the trident from Ariel. Seeing that the farmer had accepted Ariel's offer of peace, the mer-soldiers bowed to her respectfully. Then they too offered up their tridents.

The farmers and the fisherman quickly freed the mer-soldier from the fishing net. Then the one who had accepted Ariel's trident ran back to the fields. When he returned, his arms were full of wildflowers and stalks of grain.

"These are for you," he said, "and your people—from us, your new friends!"

Back at the palace, Ariel presented her father with the gifts from the surface world, and told him all about the peaceful encounter with the humans. At first, King Triton was angry with her for putting herself in such danger. Then his soldiers told him how courageous Ariel had been, and he couldn't help but feel proud.

"Bringing peace between two worlds is a noble feat, indeed," said the sea king. "But you are not to visit the surface again. Do you understand me?"

"I won't go up there again," said Ariel, giving her father a hug.

For at least a week, she added silently.

DISNEY'S
THE
LION KING
A Day Without Pumbaa

"**M**mm!" said Timon. "Breakfast time! Come to daddy, you tasty little critters."

Timon was showing Simba how to catch the plentiful but sneaky bugs that crept and flew throughout the jungle.

"Too bad Pumbaa has to miss out on this feast," Timon said. "I haven't seen him since sunup. Have you? Ooh! There's a good one! Quiet now. . . . Watch me, Simba—and learn!"

Timon crouched stealthily behind a rotting log crawling with beetles. He was just about to leap, when—"AAARGH!"

Without any warning at all, Pumbaa came hurtling out of the treetops, swinging wildly on a vine . . . straight into Timon. In an instant, Timon was a meerkat pancake.

"Oops . . . sorry, Timon," Pumbaa said.

"Sorry!" fumed Timon. "*Sorry*, you say! That's the nineteenth—no, the *twentieth* time you've crashed into me this week!"

"But it wasn't on purpose," Pumbaa told him.

"You never do anything on purpose," Timon replied. "You're a *natural* disaster! Why, you couldn't catch a bug if it flew into your mouth."

"That's not true!" Pumbaa protested. "Look! I'll prove it."

The clumsy warthog lunged for a juicy grub, only to fall headfirst into a mud puddle—splattering Simba and Timon from head to toe.

"That's it!" cried Timon. "I've had it! No more disasters!"

Pumbaa looked heartbroken. "Do you think I'm a disaster, too?" he asked Simba.

"Well . . ." Simba began, "you have to admit, sometimes you *do* do pretty disastrous things."

Pumbaa hung his head. "You're right," he said. "Nobody wants me around. It'd be better for everyone if I just left." And with that, he slowly plodded off into the jungle.

Just then, the clouds thickened, and a bolt of lightning shot through the sky.

"Wait a second," said Simba. "Timon, we can't let him go!"

But Timon didn't even turn to look. "If that warthog thinks I'm going to beg him to stay, he's sorely mistaken. Trust me, Simba," said Timon, "he'll be back by lunchtime."

But as the rain began to pour down, Simba wasn't so sure.

The storm came and went. And so did lunch . . . and dinner. And still no Pumbaa. Simba began to worry—a lot.

"We shouldn't have been so hard on him," said the cub. "I wonder if he's okay."

"He's fine," snapped Timon, who was still sore from getting squashed that morning. "Besides, he's the one who walked out on us, remember? Poof! Gone! History, as far as I'm concerned. Pumbaa? Who's that? Never heard of him!"

Simba sighed.

"Oh, stop moping," Timon said, "and think about it. We can do anything we want now—without worrying about getting knocked down, covered with mud, or run over. Let's enjoy it."

So off they went. First, they tried chasing vultures. Then, they splashed in the river. They even tried playing a game of tag among the vines. But somehow, nothing they did seemed like very much fun. Something—or someone—was always missing.

"So, what do you want to do now?" Timon asked Simba.

"I don't know," said Simba. "What do *you* want to do?"

"I asked you first," said Timon.

The sun began to dip below the horizon. Timon sighed.
He was bored. And, he admitted to himself, it was also
possible that he missed Pumbaa, just a little.

"There's got to be something fun to do," said Simba.

"Well," said Timon gloomily, "what do you *want* to do?"

"I don't know," said Simba. "What do *you* want to do?"

And so they went on . . . and on . . . and on. And they
would have gone on even longer, if a sudden rustling along
the riverbank hadn't interrupted them.

"Timon! Simba! Look what I found!"

Like a giddy tornado, Pumbaa tumbled out of the jungle, sweeping up Timon and Simba in his wake and sending all three of them crashing into the trunk of a large tree. The bugs Pumbaa had brought for his friends went flying into the air and then hit the ground—*plop! plop! plop!*

"I'm back," Pumbaa groaned.

"So we see," mumbled Timon.

Miserably, Pumbaa stood up and faced his crumpled friends. "I came back to say I missed you," he said. "But *now* look what I've done! I'm the worst friend ever."

"Now, wait one minute!" cried Timon. "That's just not true!"

"You're a wonderful friend, and we missed you!" said Simba. "We even missed your disasters."

"It appears," said Timon wryly, "that we've grown accustomed to being stepped on, bruised, and squashed."

"You mean you're willing to put up with me?" asked Pumbaa, trying to hold back his happy tears.

"You bet!" said Simba. "You're our very favorite disaster."

DISNEY'S MULAN

Jin's Treasure

After Mulan had saved China from the Huns, her life returned, for the most part, to normal. Back in her village, she still helped out her family the way she always had, and in time, some people forgot how courageous and ingenious Fa Zhou's daughter really was.

Then one day, as Mulan was fetching water for her mother, a group of frightened children came running toward her.

"Help! Help!" they shouted. "Our friend Jin is trapped in a cave!"

"Oh, no!" exclaimed Mulan. "Hurry—take me to him! Mushu," she called to her little dragon friend, "you've got to come, too!"

The children led Mulan to the other side of the mountain. There, she found the strongest of the village men already hard at work.

"A boulder has fallen, blocking the entrance to the cave," Wang, the blacksmith, explained. "The boy ran in only seconds before it fell." Then his face hardened into a scowl. "But what are *you* doing here?" he asked Mulan. "This is no place for a girl! It will take muscles of steel to move this boulder."

"Yes!" agreed Chung, the carpenter. "Get out of our way. If you want to do something useful, go back to the village and fetch us some water." Then the men returned to their work—pulling and pushing at the boulder in vain.

33

Mulan wasted no time. She did return to the village, but not to fetch water. Instead, she found a shovel and ran back to the cave.

"That boulder is too heavy to be moved," Mulan told the men. "Let's try another way."

Wang and his friends frowned and kept on pushing.

"Come on," Mulan urged. "What do you have to lose?"

At last, the large men shook their heads and reluctantly stepped aside. Mulan began to dig at the base of the boulder.

"If you can't move an obstacle," she said, "you can always try to go around it." And slowly but surely, she formed a tunnel beneath the rock.

Once the tunnel was finished, Mulan and Mushu climbed under the boulder, into the damp darkness of the cave.

"How about some light?" Mulan asked the dragon.

"No problem!" replied Mushu, opening his mouth and belching out a flame that lit up the whole cave. And there was Jin!

"Boy, am I happy to see you!" the boy exclaimed as he ran up to meet them.

"We're happy to see you, too!" said Mulan. "But what made you come in here? Don't you know caves can be dangerous?"

"I know," said Jin. "But I saw something shiny, and I wanted to know what it was."

Mulan looked around. "You mean *that*?"

There, in the back of the cave, lit up by Mushu's fire, was not just one shiny object—but many! The cave was full of hidden treasure! Mushu was so stunned, he almost swallowed his own flames.

"Think of what this fortune could mean for our village!" exclaimed Mulan as Jin climbed happily onto the shimmering mountain of gold, jewels, and precious vases. "Come on!" Jin said. "Let's go show the others." Then they each grabbed an armful of treasure and headed for the tunnel.

As the pair emerged, followed by Mushu, the crowd let out a cheer. "Mulan did it!" they all shouted. Then they noticed the gold and jewels.

"What have you found?" asked Wang.

"It's a treasure," she told him. "And there's more of it inside. Much more! Now I can go back to the village and fetch some water," she continued, grinning. "I'm pretty thirsty after all that digging."

Wang and the other men lowered their eyes. How foolish they had been, thinking Mulan could not help them just because she was a girl!

"Forgive us," said Wang. "If it weren't for you, Jin would still be trapped. You are a great hero."

"Let's just get this treasure back to the village," said Mulan, blushing, "and celebrate our newfound fortune!"

Soon, all the treasure was collected from the cave, and a great feast was prepared—with Mulan and Mushu as the guests of honor. The great gong was rung, and the whole village turned out to show their gratitude to Mulan, not just for bringing them riches, but for saving one of their children.

In the years that followed, the villagers put their new fortune to much good use. Houses were built for the poor; new schools were built for the children; roads were repaired; and enough food was stored that no one would ever go hungry again. And the tale of Mulan's heroism was written down for all to read, so they would never again forget her courage and wisdom.

THE ARISTOCATS

The Coziest Carriage

One day, for a treat, O'Malley took Duchess and her kittens down to the junkyard to visit O'Malley's old and dear friend, Scat Cat. Scat Cat lived in a broken-down carriage that had once been very grand indeed.

"This carriage used to belong to a viscount," Scat Cat told Berlioz, Toulouse, and Marie. "And before that, to an archduke." But the wheels had fallen apart long ago, and the cushions were sunken and shredded. To top it all off, there was an enormous hole right in the middle of the worn, tattered roof.

Still, as far as Scat Cat was concerned, his home could not have been more perfect. "I feel free here," he told the kittens. "I can come and go as I please. And when I stretch out on the cushions at night, I look up and there are the stars, a-twinklin' and a-winkin' back at me!"

The kittens had a grand time playing with Scat Cat in the junkyard. But when the sun went down, they were glad to return to the soft pillows, cozy blankets, and warm milk waiting for them back at Madame Bonfamille's mansion.

But a few days later, who should appear at Madame's doorstep but Scat Cat himself.

"You'll never believe it," he said. "I went into town to stretch my legs, and when I got back . . . *poof!* The carriage was gone!"

"Well, naturally," said Duchess, "you will have to stay with us! I'm sure Madame would be delighted to have you as our guest."

"Oh, goody! Goody!" cheered the kittens.

"Well . . ." Scat Cat said, thinking it over. "That's a mighty nice invitation. Don't mind if I do."

But after only one night, Scat Cat began to feel blue. The life of a house cat just wasn't for him. Everything at Madame Bonfamille's happened according to a schedule. Meals were at eight o'clock, noon, and six o'clock sharp. Naps were from nine to eleven in the morning, and one to four in the afternoon.

And outings always began at four-thirty in Madame's car. Scat Cat missed coming and going as he pleased.

"But you know what I miss most?" Scat Cat told O'Malley and the kittens. "My old carriage. What I wouldn't give to be able to look up at the sky and count the twinklin' stars as I drift off to sleep on those lumpy, worn-out cushions. . . ."

Scat was homesick.

"I wish there was some way we could get that carriage back for him," Marie said to her brothers later that day.

"Maybe there is!" Berlioz replied with a grin. "Follow me!"

Soon, the
kittens arrived
at the carriage
house.

For a while now,
Madame had been complaining
about her old carriage. No matter
how many times she repaired it, the rear
wheel kept coming off its axle; the gold paint was
peeling off in sheets; and the canvas top had begun
to sag and fray. "I'm embarrassed to be seen in it,"
Berlioz had heard her say. "It's not even worth repairing."

With this in mind, Berlioz climbed into the old carriage, unfurled his claws,
and gleefully pounced on the old upholstery.

"Come on! Dig in!" he said.

So Toulouse and Marie joined him, and in no time at all, the kittens had
those cushions looking like the ones in Scat Cat's old carriage.

"Don't forget the roof!" Marie reminded her brothers. The kittens raced up to the top of the carriage, where they jumped and bounced to their hearts' content. Finally, after a triple backward somersault with one and a half twists, Toulouse came crashing down through the carriage roof, making a hole the size of Madame's parasol.

"Hooray!" cheered Marie.

"Oh, my!" exclaimed a voice. The kittens turned, and there was Madame, with her chauffeur. She surveyed the damage . . . and smiled! "At last I have an excuse to buy a new carriage," she said to the chauffeur. "Take this one out to the junkyard at once."

"I don't believe it!" cried Scat Cat, when the kittens led him to his new home, back in the junkyard. "These seats are even more torn up than the ones in my old carriage. And look at the size of that hole in the roof. It's *purr*-fect! How can I ever thank you?" he asked the kittens.

"It was our pleasure," said Berlioz. He flexed his claws. "It's not every day we're thanked for clawing something to pieces!"